THE BOXCAR CHILDREN
SURPRISE ISLAND
THE YELLOW HOUSE MYSTERY
MYSTERY RANCH
MIKE'S MYSTERY
BLUE BAY MYSTERY
THE WOODSHED MYSTERY
THE LIGHTHOUSE MYSTERY
MOUNTAIN TOP MYSTERY
SCHOOLHOUSE MYSTERY
CABOOSE MYSTERY
HOUSEBOAT MYSTERY
SNOWBOUND MYSTERY
TREE HOUSE MYSTERY
BICYCLE MYSTERY
MYSTERY IN THE SAND
MYSTERY BEHIND THE WALL
BUS STATION MYSTERY
BENNY UNCOVERS A MYSTERY
THE HAUNTED CABIN MYSTERY
THE DESERTED LIBRARY MYSTERY
THE ANIMAL SHELTER MYSTERY
THE OLD MOTEL MYSTERY
THE MYSTERY OF THE HIDDEN
   PAINTING
THE AMUSEMENT PARK MYSTERY
THE MYSTERY OF THE MIXED-UP ZOO
THE CAMP-OUT MYSTERY
THE MYSTERY GIRL
THE MYSTERY CRUISE
THE DISAPPEARING FRIEND MYSTERY
THE MYSTERY OF THE SINGING GHOST
THE MYSTERY IN THE SNOW
THE PIZZA MYSTERY
THE MYSTERY HORSE
THE MYSTERY AT THE DOG SHOW
THE CASTLE MYSTERY
THE MYSTERY OF THE LOST VILLAGE
THE MYSTERY ON THE ICE
THE MYSTERY OF THE PURPLE POOL
THE GHOST SHIP MYSTERY

T...
THE ...
THE MYSTERY OF THE HIDDEN BEACH
THE MYSTERY OF THE MISSING CAT
THE MYSTERY AT SNOWFLAKE INN
THE MYSTERY ON STAGE
THE DINOSAUR MYSTERY
THE MYSTERY OF THE STOLEN MUSIC
THE MYSTERY AT THE BALL PARK
THE CHOCOLATE SUNDAE MYSTERY
THE MYSTERY OF THE HOT
   AIR BALLOON
THE MYSTERY BOOKSTORE
THE PILGRIM VILLAGE MYSTERY
THE MYSTERY OF THE STOLEN
   BOXCAR
THE MYSTERY IN THE CAVE
THE MYSTERY ON THE TRAIN
THE MYSTERY AT THE FAIR
THE MYSTERY OF THE LOST MINE
THE GUIDE DOG MYSTERY
THE HURRICANE MYSTERY
THE PET SHOP MYSTERY
THE MYSTERY OF THE SECRET MESSAGE
THE FIREHOUSE MYSTERY
THE MYSTERY IN SAN FRANCISCO
THE NIAGARA FALLS MYSTERY
THE MYSTERY AT THE ALAMO
THE OUTER SPACE MYSTERY
THE SOCCER MYSTERY
THE MYSTERY IN THE OLD ATTIC
THE GROWLING BEAR MYSTERY
THE MYSTERY OF THE LAKE MONSTER
THE MYSTERY AT PEACOCK HALL
THE WINDY CITY MYSTERY
THE BLACK PEARL MYSTERY
THE CEREAL BOX MYSTERY
THE PANTHER MYSTERY
THE MYSTERY OF THE QUEEN'S JEWELS
THE STOLEN SWORD MYSTERY
THE BASKETBALL MYSTERY

The Boxcar Children Mysteries

THE MYSTERY OF THE STOLEN SNOWBOARD

created by
GERTRUDE CHANDLER WARNER

ALBERT WHITMAN & Company
Chicago, Illinois

Library of Congress Cataloging-in-Publication Data

Warner, Gertrude Chandler.
The mystery of the stolen snowboard / by Gertrude Chandler Warner ; interior
illustrations by Anthony VanArsdale.
pages cm. — (The Boxcar children mysteries ; 134)
Summary: "The winter sports season is here, and the Aldens are excited
about all the snow activities—especially snowboarding. But soon they find
themselves in the middle of a mystery surrounding a star athlete and
a stolen snowboard"—Provided by publisher.
ISBN 978-0-8075-8728-7 (hardback) — ISBN 978-0-8075-8729-4 (paperback)
[1. Mystery and detective stories 2. Brothers and sisters—Fiction. 3. Orphans—
Fiction. 4. Snowboarding—Fiction.] I. VanArsdale, Anthony, illustrator. II. Title.
PZ7.W244Muer 2014
[Fic]—dc23   2013033071

10 9 8 7 6 5 4 3 2 1 LB 18 17 16 15 14 13

Cover art by Gideon Kendall.
Interior illustrations by Anthony VanArsdale.

For more information about Albert Whitman & Company,
visit our web site at www.albertwhitman.com.

Contents

THE MYSTERY OF THE STOLEN SNOWBOARD

CHAPTER I

Hidden Hills

"Turn here." Henry Alden checked the map. "We need to take a left on Evergreen Road."

"There's no sign," Grandfather Alden said. "Are you certain?" Henry had been directing them through the rugged mountains for the past hour. The GPS didn't work because they had no phone service.

"I think that big tree marks the street," Henry told Grandfather.

"An evergreen pine." Jessie pushed back

her long brown hair and pointed at the tree, its thick branches dripping with heavy snow. "That makes sense."

"I wish there was a real street sign," six-year-old Benny said from the backseat. "I don't want to get lost." He shivered. "How much longer?" A loud grumbling sound came from his tummy.

Jessie was twelve, six years older than Benny. She held his hand to make him feel better. "We'll be there soon," she told him. "Don't worry."

"I'm not worried," Benny said. "I'm hungry." He stared out the window at the lightly falling snow and frowned.

"You're always hungry," Jessie said with a laugh. She handed him a small bag filled with raisins.

While Benny snacked, Henry reviewed the map again. "I'm positive this is the correct way." They made another turn at a large rock. "Clayton warned me that it was hard to find the town."

"Hidden Hills sure is hidden." Violet

looked up from her art and straightened her pigtails. She'd just finished quick sketches of the snowy pine tree and ice-covered rock. Although she was only ten years old, Violet was a keen observer and saw details that others sometimes missed. Glancing down at her sketch pad, Violet made sure she had drawn the angle of the sun correctly. She erased one line and fixed another to get it perfect.

"The town should be around this next bend," Henry said. Grandfather took a slow turn to the right and crossed over a short bridge with a frozen river underneath.

"Look!" Jessie leaned up in her seat and read the small sign ahead of them. "*Established 1882.*" She'd read about Hidden Hills on the Internet. Jessie liked to research. "This used to be a mining town," she told the others. "There were silver mines all over the area."

"And now it's home to the first Super Snowboard Classic." At fourteen, Henry was usually much more mature than his brother or sisters, but seeing a few small buildings in the distance, he clapped his hands and cheered. "This is very exciting. I'm glad Clayton invited us to see him snowboard this weekend. It's going to be so much fun!"

Henry Alden and Clayton Hollow had met at school in Greenfield. They'd been keeping in touch since Clayton left town to travel the globe, competing to become one of the greatest teenage snowboarders in the world. When he announced that he was coming to Hidden Hills, Henry asked Grandfather if they could go. The mountain town was only a few hours' drive from home and this was an important tournament. The top four snowboarders would qualify for a brand-new elite training camp.

Watch, Jessie's wire-haired terrier, had come along too. He was in the backseat next to Benny. They were sitting with their noses pressed against the window. "It's cold out there, Henry," Benny reported as his breath fogged up the glass.

"Snowboarding is a winter sport." Henry passed Benny a scarf and hat. "It's supposed to be cold."

"I wish Clayton liked summer sports," Benny said. "We could have gone to the beach instead."

Jessie giggled. "We can get some hot chocolate right after we check into the hotel if you want."

"And cookies?" Benny asked.

"Of course." Jessie ruffled her brother's dark brown hair.

Violet sharpened a fresh black charcoal pencil, then made new pictures of each of the shops they saw: a bakery, a bank, a restaurant called Burger Bonanza, the Coffee Hut, a medical clinic, and finally, at the end of the street, a three-story redbrick hotel. She looked around for other stores to put into her sketch pad. "Is that it?" she asked. "Where's the rest of the city?"

"You've seen it all," Henry replied. "Some houses are tucked away behind the trees. There's a school and a grocery store about thirty miles away in the next town."

"Greenfield used to be a small town, just like this," Grandfather said. "It was a long

time ago, before any of you children were born, but I remember when I was a child, there was only one paved street."

"I don't believe you!" Benny exclaimed, his eyes wide. "No way!"

"It's true," Grandfather said. "When we get back home, I'll show you pictures."

Jessie, Violet, Henry, and Benny lived with their grandfather. After their parents died, they had run away and hid in a railroad boxcar in the woods. They heard that Grandfather Alden was mean. Even though they'd never met him, they were afraid. But when he finally found the children, they discovered he wasn't mean at all. Now the children lived with him, and their boxcar was a clubhouse in the backyard.

"We're here." Grandfather parked the car in front of the hotel. "Let's go check into our rooms."

While they gathered their bags, a man in a heavy coat and earmuffs under a wool hat came rushing toward them. "Get out of town!" he shouted. "Go away."

Henry pushed his brown hair out of his eyes and stepped forward. "Excuse me?" he asked politely. "I don't understand. We're here for the snowboarding competition—"

"You aren't welcome!" The man forced a yellow flyer into Henry's hands. He poked a long finger at the printed words. "Majestic Mountain must be stopped! Read this and you'll understand why."

Henry glanced down and scanned it. "What's Majestic Mountain?"

"It's the worst idea in history," the man said, stomping his boot. "Name's Ralph Fellows," he said, introducing himself. "I own the Coffee Hut, but more importantly, I'm also president of the Save Hidden Hills Committee."

"Nice to meet you, Mr. Fellows." Jessie held out her hand to shake his.

He pulled back, shoving a flyer into her hand instead. "The organizers of this snowboard event want to create their training camp right here in Hidden Hills. Just imagine it! They'll ruin the environment."

He gave Benny, Violet, and Grandfather flyers too. "Snowboarding will be just the beginning. They'll cut down the trees to make more hotels, chase away the animals to make more slopes for skiing, and carve away ancient rock formations for an ice-skating rink. More activities mean more restaurants. That means trash, terrible traffic, crowded shops, and"—he gasped and lowered his voice—"they even want to build an airport."

"But what's Majestic Mountain?" Benny repeated Henry's question.

"He wrote about it on the flyer," Jessie told Benny after scanning the page. "If there's a permanent training camp here, the city won't be called Hidden Hills anymore. The people in charge want to change the name to Majestic Mountain." She glanced down at the flyer. "Mr. Fellows wrote that in the 1800s when the silver mines were all used up, the miners hitched their horses and moved away. They left their trash, rusted equipment, and broken, deserted shacks behind."

"Took a hundred years to clean it up and

another hundred for the trees to grow back," Mr. Fellows said. "If this place becomes a sporting town, it'll never be the same!" He moaned. "Now get out of here. You *have* to go away."

Grandfather moved between Mr. Fellows and the children. "You are entitled to your opinion," he said. "But you cannot threaten us."

Mr. Fellows was about to reply when two people came running out of the hotel.

"Stop!" a man shouted. He was wearing a heavy coat with *Sheriff* printed on the back and waving a badge. "Stop! Police!"

"Hiya, Tommy." Mr. Fellows turned and greeted the officer casually as though they'd known each other a long time.

"There he is." The hotel manager was with the sheriff. "I saw him at the hotel. Ralph Fellows was the one who threw the paint." She pointed at Mr. Fellows. "There is a display of the plans for Majestic Mountain and the new snowboard training camp in the lobby. I watched him mess up the drawings and vandalize the model buildings."

"You've gone too far this time, Ralph," the sheriff said. "We've known each other for years, but you know I can't let you get away with wrecking other people's property. I'm going to have to take you down to the station." The sheriff stepped forward, holding out a pair of handcuffs.

Mr. Fellows began to laugh. His deep, rumbling laughter echoed off the tall, snow-covered mountains. "Be sure to recycle those flyers," he told the Aldens. Then he ran down the street.

CHAPTER 2

Stolen!

After checking into their room, Jessie, Violet, and Benny went to get hot chocolate, while Henry headed toward the snowboarding slope. He wanted to catch up with Clayton.

When he passed through the lobby, Henry noticed that the mess Mr. Fellows had made was all cleaned up. Whatever paint he'd tossed around was washable. The trash was gone and everything seemed in place. The hotel manager, Martha, smiled and waved at Henry as he went outside.

Henry easily found his friend standing at the bottom of the only chairlift in Hidden Hills. Clayton was wearing ski pants, a heavy jacket, and thick boots, and his long blond hair stuck out from under his bright orange helmet. His snowboard leaned against a nearby wooden fence.

"Hi. I'm so glad you made it," Clayton said. "You're just in time. I'm heading up for the first run of the day."

Henry raised a hand over his eyes to better see the slope of the mountain in front of them. "Looks dangerous," he commented. "That's a steep trail coming down."

"This is one of the most difficult mountain terrains in the world," Clayton said. "It's got a long vertical slope, where we do the racing events, but it also has a great half-pipe." He pointed to a spot about halfway up the mountain where the snow had been carved out to look like a big letter *U*.

Henry had seen Clayton boarding on the half-pipe in Internet videos. Sliding from edge to edge, Clayton would gain speed and then do spins and tricks as he soared off the open walls of the U.

Clayton was so good he even had a flip combo named after him—the Hollow. It was amazing to watch.

Jessie, Violet, and Benny joined them with their cups of hot chocolate. Violet was holding Watch's leash.

"Are you going to do the Swallow trick today?" Benny asked Clayton.

Henry laughed. "It's Hollow, Benny. The trick is named after Clayton's last name."

"Oh good," Benny said, raising his cup to his lips. "We can name a swallow trick after me then." He took a big sip of hot chocolate and gulped it down. "De-li-cious!"

Everyone laughed.

"You keep practicing, Benny," Clayton told him. He grabbed his snowboard. "I better go. The first race is about to begin. I really want to win a spot in the training camp."

"Good luck," Benny told him.

"We're doing an event today called a slalom," Clayton explained. "I need to go as fast as I can down the mountain and zigzag between thirty different flagpoles. Each snowboarder takes a turn. Then the fastest time wins the race."

"We'll be watching—" Violet began but then Watch started barking at a girl dressed in snowboarding clothes. She was carrying a shiny bright pink board.

"Hurry up, Clayton," the girl said, pushing past him toward the chairlift. "We need to get to the starting gate." The girl pointed at a large man in a black jacket standing at the top of the chairlift. "My coach expects me to win one of the camp spots. You know there are only four places and five snowboarders. Not everyone will get a spot."

"You're a great snowboarder, Mercedes," Clayton said with a laugh. "You've been training since the day you were born. Coach McNaught should stop nagging you. You'll go to the elite camp for sure."

"Coach warned that you might beat me today." She placed her helmet over her shoulder-length dark hair and tightened the strap. "I think he's trying to scare me."

"Is it working?" Clayton asked. He narrowed his eyes and snarled. "If I scare you, do you think you might fall and lose some points? Maybe hit a flag?" He smiled. "I mean, I don't want you to get hurt, but I'd love to see my name above yours on the scoreboard."

"Fat chance." Mercedes laughed. "I'll beat you in both events today. I'm feeling lucky." And with that, she jumped onto the chairlift and headed up the mountain.

"Wow," Henry said, letting out a big breath. "She's mean."

Clayton smiled. "Nah. She's teasing me. Mercedes is my friend."

Henry took one last look at Mercedes's new shiny board as the chairlift carried her up the mountain. Clayton's yellow board, on the other hand, was dented and scratched. It was old and had little chips out of the side.

Jessie said, "I recognized her. Mercedes Moon is a really popular snowboarder. She's been on magazine covers and has videos all over the Internet."

"She can't be better than you, Clayton," Benny said. "You're the best snowboarder I know."

"I work hard at it," Clayton replied. "I'm not the best yet, but if I can get into the training camp—I might be someday." He went on, saying, "All the boarders here are pretty equal in skill." Clayton put on his gloves. "But, out of everyone, Mercedes will be the toughest one to beat. Her parents spend a lot of money on her training. Her coach is a world champion gold medalist. And Mercedes uses the most expensive equipment." He tapped a finger on his board. "Of course, I have Yellow Bessie, here, and maybe, just maybe, Mercedes is wrong. It might turn out that today is *my* lucky day!"

An empty chair came around the lift. Clayton jumped on it and waved as he moved up the mountain toward the starting gate.

The Aldens headed for the viewing area at the side of the slope. From their seats on metal stadium benches, the Aldens had a great view of the whole mountain.

Suddenly, Benny screamed and jumped up from the bench. "Augh!" He dropped his hot chocolate to the ground below and it immediately melted the snow.

"What's going on?" Henry asked Benny. He picked up Benny's cup and tossed it into the trash.

"There! Over there!" Benny could barely catch his breath. His finger shook as he pointed to the trees across from where they were standing. "Did you see it, Henry? Did you, Violet? How about you, Jessie?"

"No," they all said. "We didn't see anything."

"Did you see it, Watch?" Benny asked.

The dog flopped down in the snow and looked bored.

"You have to believe me," Benny told them all. "Over there—on the other side of the snowboard slope—there was a yeti! It was like Bigfoot, only all white." His voice dropped to a whisper. "I saw a TV show all about yetis.

They are these huge hairy monsters that some people think live in snowy mountain areas"—he looked around—"just like Hidden Hills." He went on, "Most people think yetis are just legends, but now I *know* they exist."

"I don't know…" Jessie said, putting a hand over her eyes to see farther into the woods.

"Well, whatever it was," Henry said, "It's gone now." He squinted toward the trees then raised his head toward the mountaintop. "Here comes Clayton."

Clayton Hollow rocketed down the mountain.

Everyone was cheering, stomping, and making noise.

Red and blue triangle flags were planted close together. Clayton turned tightly, tipping on the edge of his snowboard as he rotated around each one. Jessie and Violet were jumping up and down and clapping their hands as Clayton sped down the course. Henry was shouting, "Go! Go! Go!"

"Wow! That was fast," Benny said when

Clayton reached the bottom. He hadn't even had time to eat a whole piece of beef jerky before the race was over.

The cheering fans went wild when Clayton whipped off his hat and slowed to a stop near the chairlift.

"That was exciting," Violet said.

"Here comes the next racer," Henry said, looking back up at the mountaintop. "It's Mercedes."

Mercedes and the other snowboarders each took their turns on the course. The boarders were fast and skilled. The Aldens cheered for them, but they all really hoped Clayton would win.

After the race, the competing snowboarders gathered at the bottom of the mountain and stacked their boards by the chairlift. Clayton left his helmet sitting in the snow, and they walked together to see their official speeds and final ranks. Each snowboarder's score would be added together at the end of the third race, and the four boarders with the highest scores would get to go to the camp.

Mercedes had a perfect run and came in first place.

Clayton came in second. His time was only one second behind hers.

Patricia Gutierrez and Jasper Novak took third and fourth place.

Hyun Lee had hit an icy patch halfway down and missed two important turns. He lost a lot of points and finished last.

"Congratulations," Jessie told Clayton. "Second place!"

"I'm really happy," Clayton said with a grin. "It was a fantastic morning!

"I feel bad about Hyun," he added. "But he's younger than me. If he doesn't make it this year, he can go to the training camp next year. They aren't taking anyone older than fifteen, so this is my only chance." He held up crossed fingers. "Let's hope I do well in the next race!"

"I drew a picture of you coming down the mountain." Violet showed him her art. Clayton looked like a blur in the center of the white page. "It's kind of messy," she said, pointing to the lines she drew to show the wind off his orange helmet.

"I love it," Clayton said, taking the artwork. "Thanks."

Benny noticed Mercedes walking away from the chairlift with her pink snowboard. It was the first time he'd seen her since the race. He rushed over and stopped her.

"You were very speedy today," he said. "Good job." He held out his bag of beef jerky. "I bet all that exercise made you hungry. Want a snack?"

"No thanks. I'm a vegetarian." Mercedes smiled at him, but her smile faded when a man approached. "My coach is coming," she said with a groan.

Her coach was tall. He towered over Benny, who barely reached the man's waist. "Your start was slow," the coach told Mercedes, stepping between her and Benny. "You could have shaved another second off your time at the third pole," he said. "And what did I tell you about hanging around after a race?"

He glared at Mercedes. "Do not speak to

the competition," the coach said before she could answer. "You shouldn't talk to the friends of other athletes either," he added. He pulled her away from Benny. "We need to prepare for the Snowboard Cross event. That race starts in two hours. You must have a bigger gap between you and Clayton. One second is too close."

As she followed her coach toward the hotel, Mercedes dropped her glove near Jessie. Jessie reached down to get it, but Mercedes got there first. As their heads were near each other, Mercedes whispered, "I have plans that my coach doesn't know about." She winked. "Big plans. You'll see."

Jessie didn't understand. "I—" she started, but Mercedes was already gone.

"Forget about Mercedes," Hyun told Jessie. "We rarely see her after a race and she never hangs out." He took off his helmet. His brown hair was cut short. There was sweat from the early race on his forehead. "We'll grab our boards and we can get a snack at the Coffee Hut."

While Hyun, Jasper, Patricia, and Clayton went to get their snowboards, Jessie, Henry, Violet, and Benny waited for them near the scoreboard.

Suddenly they heard a boy shout, "No! No! No!" from near the chairlift. It sounded like Clayton.

The Aldens ran over to see what was happening.

"It's gone!" Clayton said, pointing at three snowboards leaning on the wooden fence. "My snowboard is missing!"

CHAPTER 3

It's a Mystery

A small crowd gathered around the empty spot where Clayton's board had been. Clayton was surrounded by the other snowboarders, the organizers of the snowboard competition, and the sheriff.

Jessie, Henry, Benny, and Violet stood to the side, out of the way, discussing how they could help. The Aldens were good at solving mysteries. The minute Clayton discovered his snowboard was missing, Jessie had taken a journal and pen from her purse to record notes. Henry was looking for clues while Violet checked for footprints.

Benny took Watch by the leash and told the dog, "Come on, boy. Sniff out the thief."

Watch looked up at Benny then sat down.

"No scent to follow, huh?" Benny patted Watch on the head. "First you didn't see the yeti. Now you can't find the thief." He bent down and stared directly into Watch's eyes. "You feeling okay?"

Watch popped up and licked Benny's nose.

"Ewww." Benny wiped dog slobber off his face and said, "All right. You can rest now, but when you find something, you better start barking like crazy."

"Coming through..." A woman carrying a black snowboard pushed her way through the crowd to the fence. "Out of my way." She reached Clayton and shoved the board toward him. "Here. Take this."

Clayton stared at the board for a long moment. "No, thank you."

"You don't have any other options," the lady said. "If you aren't on the mountain when the race starts, they'll run it without you." She tapped her wristwatch. "You have less than two hours to get ready."

"I know the rules," Clayton said with a sigh. He looked again at the snowboard the lady was offering. It was brand new. The dark paint glistened against the white snow and made the words painted on the front stand out like a billboard.

Burger Bonanza.

"Who is that?" Violet whispered to Jessie, nodding toward the lady. Jessie shrugged.

Hyun was standing nearby and overheard Violet's question.

"That's Laura Taylor. She owns the Burger Bonanza. Ms. Taylor is president of the Hidden Hills Elite Training Camp Committee. It was her idea to have the competition here. The deal she made with the developers was that they could put in as many hotels and ski slopes as they wanted, but she would own any new restaurants that opened in town. They'll all have *Bonanza* in their names. Breakfast Bonanza. Bakery Bonanza...like that."

"Banana Bonanza, Brownie Bonanza, Broccoli Bonanza..." Benny's eyes grew wide. "Bacon Bonanza!" He rubbed his belly.

"Since she would own the only restaurants in town, she'd be rich," Hyun said. "Richer, I mean. She's already really rich."

When Hyun finished, Henry asked, "Why does she have a Burger Bonanza snowboard?"

"She wants to sponsor the group at the

training camp," he replied. "We'd all wear the restaurant logo on our hats and jackets and boards."

"You'd be big, walking commercials," Benny remarked.

"Most athletes have sponsors," Hyun explained. "Watch any sport and you'll see the names of the companies that give the athletes shoes and equipment. Companies even buy the playing fields."

"Hmmm. Watching a commercial on TV or reading an advertisement in a magazine is okay." Benny considered the idea of having a sponsor. "Even if I was really good at sports, I don't think I'd want to *be* a commercial for a company."

"If we wear her clothing and use her snowboards, Ms. Taylor and Burger Bonanza will give us all free food," Hyun said. "As much as we want."

"Well, then that settles it!" Benny said. "Free burgers and fries until my tummy is stuffed? Give me a Bonanza hat. I'll wear it."

"You're never stuffed." Jessie laughed. "You

can't eat there all the time, Benny. It's not very healthy."

"I could if it was yummy," Benny said.

"That's the problem," Hyun said. "Clayton doesn't like Burger Bonanza."

Just then, the Aldens heard Clayton tell Ms. Taylor, "Your food is bad for people. Why would I let the kids who watch me snowboard think I enjoy eating there? There isn't even a salad on your menu and the burgers have fried stuff all over them." He shook his head. "I'd rather never snowboard again than ride your Burger Bonanza board."

"Have it your way," Ms. Taylor huffed. "You are the only one here who refuses to have Burger Bonanza sponsor the group. The only one!" She glared at him. Anger made her cheeks red and puffy. "I hope you never find your snowboard."

Before Ms. Taylor even turned the corner, Jessie whipped out her notebook and wrote down Ms. Taylor's name on a blank page. "We have our first suspect," she said.

"We actually have two suspects," Violet

said. She reminded Jessie about what had happened when they first came into town. "Mr. Fellows seems like the type of guy who will do anything to stop the training camp and town development. Maybe he took Clayton's snowboard in order to end the competition."

"If he's the thief, then he didn't know the rule that they will race without Clayton," Henry said, rubbing his chin as he thought about Mr. Fellows.

"Maybe he plans to take other boards too?" Violet said. "He seems really determined to stop the place from becoming Majestic Mountain."

Jessie wrote Mr. Fellows's name in her notebook. "Two suspects." She turned to a blank page. "Now we need some clues."

"Wait!" Benny said. "There's another suspect."

"Who?" Jessie asked.

"The yeti, of course," Benny said.

"Why would a yeti take Clayton's snowboard?" Henry asked.

Benny pointed to one of his small feet. "It's

obvious," he said. "Walking with those big feet takes too long to get anywhere."

"I see your point..." Henry nodded, and Benny was very glad his brother understood.

"Write down the yeti, please," Benny told Jessie.

Jessie turned back to the suspect's page. She wrote *yeti* in thick letters so Benny could read them.

"Thanks, Jessie," Benny said with a small smile.

"Three suspects," Henry said. "Now we need some clues."

They all went to talk to Clayton.

"We're going to find your snowboard," Benny told him.

"I hope so." Clayton was grateful for the help. "If I don't race today, I'd have to come in first place tomorrow to make up for the lost points when they add all the scores together. If I can beat Mercedes at the half-pipe, I think I could still make the top four."

"I understand why you won't use the Burger Bonanza board," Jessie told him. "But why won't you borrow someone else's? Someone must have a snowboard they can lend you."

"Without Yellow Bessie, I *can't* possibly win. She's my good luck charm." Clayton looked very sad. "Whoever stole her knew how important she is to me. I've used that same snowboard since my first lesson on the bunny slope."

"Don't worry. We'll find Bessie." Henry put his arm around his friend's shoulders. "The Aldens are on the case."

CHAPTER 4

Plenty of Suspects

"Can I borrow a piece of paper and a pen?" Violet asked Jessie. "I've already used all the pages in my sketch pad. I'll need to get a new notebook when we get home."

"Here." Jessie tore out a page from her notebook and gave Violet an extra pen.

"Thanks." Violet quickly drew the fence at the bottom of the big mountain where they'd last seen Clayton's snowboard. Careful not to interrupt Violet's work, Henry waited until she was finished then he took a close look at the fence.

"There are no paint chips or scratch marks," he reported before checking the snow. "And with so many people stomping their boots around here, if there were any unusual footprints, they are gone now." He bent low to look at a smooth, broad marking. "There are also a lot of these snowboard tracks, but that's not strange either. The competitors rode their boards all around this area."

Keeping his eyes on the ground, Henry walked slowly to the scoreboard. "We came this way to check the snowboarding scores." He scanned the ground and the area all around. "Then we went back to the fence." Henry shrugged. "No snowboard. No clues."

Violet added the mountain and the chairlift to her drawing of the area. "Maybe," she suggested, "whoever took the snowboard jumped on the chairlift to get away."

Henry considered the idea. "That would explain how they disappeared so fast."

He rushed over to the chairlift operator. She was a young girl about Henry's age. "Hi," he said. "We're trying to help Clayton

Hollow find his missing snowboard. Were you working the chairlift when the snowboard was stolen?"

"No," the girl said, tucking her two long brown braids behind her ears. "I was taking a break at the Coffee Hut. The chairlift closed right after the race."

"No one went up or down?" Jessie asked, tapping her pen on her notebook. "Are you sure?"

"Positive," she replied. "Tell Clayton I'm rooting for him to win a spot at camp. I hope he finds his snowboard." In a low voice she added, "And I agree about Burger Bonanza. He's right not to let Ms. Taylor bully him into representing them." She stuck out her tongue. "The food there will clog your arteries and give you a heart attack."

"We'll pass the message," Henry said before they walked away. "He'll be glad you're a fan."

"Can we stop for a minute?" Benny asked when they'd taken only a few steps. "My toes are cold and I'm hungry."

Jessie checked her watch. "We don't have much time before the next race begins."

"Maybe we can just get a new hot chocolate?" Benny asked, raising both eyebrows. "That wouldn't take long. And it would be warm and delicious."

"Okay," Jessie said. "A quick drink, then we'll eat lunch after the race."

"Linner," Benny corrected. "We're already missing lunch, and it'll be too early for dinner. So we can have linner."

"I think Grandfather would like to have linner with us," Violet said. "We're supposed to call him after the race."

"I love breakfast, brunch, lunch, and dinner. But linner is my favorite," Benny said. "Oh and be-tack."

"Be-tack?" Henry asked.

"Bedtime snack, of course," Benny explained.

Everyone laughed.

They all hurried to the Coffee Hut. While Benny and Henry went inside to get the hot chocolate, Jessie and Violet stood outside.

Violet shivered and stuffed her hands into her pockets. She had brought gloves but it was hard taking them off every time she wanted to draw something.

Jessie had her hands in her pockets too. She blew out air and could see her breath.

"Are you two cold?" Ms. Taylor asked as she came down the street. She was taking large footsteps and looked like she was in a hurry.

"A little," Violet answered.

"If you lived here, you'd get used to it," Ms. Taylor said. "I grew up in Hidden Hills. My great-grandfather was mayor of this town when the miners were here. He loved having all those extra people around town. He wanted the town to grow and become a little city in the mountains. I'm going to make his dream come true." She looked up at the sign for the Coffee Hut. The shop was open all night. *Twenty-four hours* was written in big black letters on the window. "When I get all the different winter sports camps to come here, I'm going to buy this shop. It'll be called Coffee Bean Bonanza."

Just as she said that, the door to the coffee shop flung open and Ralph Fellows rushed into the street. "Get off my sidewalk!" he shouted at Ms. Taylor. "You're going to ruin this town."

"You're the one ruining everything!" She leaned in, very close to his face. "And it's not your sidewalk!"

"It's the sidewalk right in front of my coffee shop," he said. "That makes it mine." Mr. Fellows clamped his fingers into a tight fist.

"Should we call the sheriff?" Violet asked Jessie in a whisper. "I think they're about to get in a fight."

Jessie was preparing to run to the police station when Ms. Taylor straightened up and stepped away. "I know that you didn't get arrested for the mess you made when you threw paint on the development plans," she told Mr. Fellows. "I heard that you promised not to destroy anything else at the hotel so the sheriff let you go." She continued, "When I own this shop, you'll be banned from the store *and* the sidewalk. I'll make sure if you step foot on this cement, you'll get arrested and never be set free!"

Ms. Taylor turned to Jessie and Violet. "I don't have time for this nonsense. I need to go to work. Lunchtime at Burger Bonanza is the busiest time of the day."

When Ms. Taylor was gone, Mr. Fellows spun around and went back into the Coffee Hut. The door slammed behind him.

"That was intense," Jessie said to Violet. "They really don't like each other."

"They have very different ideas of how life should be in Hidden Hills," Violet agreed. "I can see both sides. It would be good to have more restaurants and shops and the elite training camp, but the town is also nice just the way it is."

"Unfortunately, Clayton and his snowboard might have been caught in the middle of their feud," Jessie said.

The door to the coffee shop opened and Benny and Henry hurried out. Benny had his hot chocolate and Henry brought a few granola bars to share.

"Treats!" Benny cheered as he gave the girls each one of the nature bars.

"The second snowboarding race is going to begin," Henry said, tossing out his wrapper. "I'm disappointed that Clayton can't compete, but I think we should watch anyway. Maybe we'll find a clue. We have to solve this mystery by tomorrow morning."

The viewing area was packed with people. Benny squeezed his way through the crowd to the front where he could see everything.

Coach McNaught stood near Benny for a few minutes. He was a big and strong-looking man, and Henry could easily see how he'd won so many competitions when he was younger. Clayton had said he was one of the best coaches in the world. Henry could tell the coach really wanted Mercedes to win not only today's race but the whole competition. His face was determined and his eyes focused on her at the mountaintop as she waited at the starting gate.

Clayton was standing a little ways off by the finish line. He looked very sad.

Over a loudspeaker, an announcer said the racers were ready for the snowboard cross.

In anticipation, the crowd stood up from their seats. Coach McNaught left the stands. Henry went to stand in his spot. The buzzer went off and the four competitors began to board downhill together.

For the snowboard cross, the boarders had to come down the steepest part of the mountain, leaping over several small jumps and navigating narrow turns and deep dips while trying to stay balanced and avoid crashing into each other. It was a tough race.

Henry thought that Coach McNaught had no reason to worry. From the very beginning, it was clear that in this race, Mercedes would be first. Her form was amazing. She was fast and beautiful to watch.

Benny cheered as she neared the bottom. Right behind her was Patricia, followed by Jasper and Hyun.

As Mercedes and Patricia came through a tight bend, Patricia boldly made a move to sneak past Mercedes.

The crowd went crazy, screaming and shouting, some cheering for Mercedes and others for Patricia. Watch put his paws over his ears and closed his eyes.

Just as it looked like Patricia might swing in past Mercedes and take first place, Patricia's board skidded out and she fell, tumbling a few feet down the mountain.

The crowd gasped.

"Oh no!" Benny shouted.

When Patricia came to a stop, she lay in the snow and didn't move.

The town doctor and his medical team went to help her while the others finished the race. The boarders were trained not to stop, no matter what. Mercedes, Jasper, and Hyun came across the finish line but there was no celebration.

Everyone was waiting to see if Patricia was all right.

After a short time, she stood up, and with a nurse's support, walked to the side of the racecourse. A sled was waiting to take her to the hospital clinic at the bottom of the mountain.

All eyes were on Patricia when suddenly, Benny screamed. "Yeti!" He jumped up and down and pointed. Behind Patricia's head, near the trees about halfway down the mountain, was a tall figure, covered in white fur.

Watch bolted upright and started barking and pulling at his leash.

"I told Watch to bark like crazy when he saw something important." Benny looked up at his siblings. "Listen to him now!"

Henry rubbed his eyes to clear them. "You were right, Benny," he said. "It *does* look like a yeti!"

CHAPTER 5

The Yeti

"Come on!" Benny shouted over his shoulder at Jessie, Violet, and Henry. "Hurry." He hiked up the slope toward where they had seen the yeti.

"I can't believe he's not complaining," Violet said as her feet sunk in deep snow. "It's freezing and climbing uphill is hard."

Henry took big steps with his long legs. "I'd never have thought I'd be having a hard time keeping up with Benny." He stopped and watched Benny slip between two trees.

47

"I'm breathing harder than ever."

"It's the altitude," Jessie said. "We are six thousand feet above sea level. The air is thinner here." She put on her gloves and wiggled her fingers to keep them warm.

"Benny has good lungs," Henry said, picking up the pace. "Watch too." The dog was at Benny's side.

"Look what I found!" Benny shouted from where he was stopped near some tall trees.

The Aldens hurried to him, jumping though small drifts of snow.

"Footprints," Benny said. His breath puffed out in a big smoky gust.

Violet took out the paper she'd been drawing on. She was going to make a quick sketch of the prints Benny found, but the foot size was bigger than her page. "Yikes," she said, laying the page near the footprint and stuffing her cold hands in her pockets.

Henry stepped in closer. "That one print is almost bigger than my two feet together, toe-to-heel," he said.

"It's the mark of a huge, monstrous yeti."

Benny put a hand above his eyes and squinted in the direction the footprints went.

The group followed Benny around a rock, over a fallen log, and through a small grove of snow-covered aspen trees.

The yeti's trail ended at an old mining cabin. The snow-covered wood was rotten and splintered, but it was clear that someone was living in the rundown shack. The glass on the windows was new and the cabin was fitted with two solar panels.

Henry raised his hand to knock on the door.

"No." Benny blocked Henry's hand. "If you knock, the hungry yeti will capture us all and eat us for dessert."

"This isn't the witch's house in *Hansel and Gretel*," Henry said.

"I wish it was. I'd break in by eating off the front door," Benny told him.

Henry gave a small laugh. "I think we should use our manners, even if we are going to meet a hungry yeti," he said and knocked.

There was no answer.

"I'll check around back." Jessie took Watch around the rear of the cabin to peek in a window. She came back a minute later. "There's no one here."

"But the footprints end at the door," Benny said, scratching his head. "The yeti has to be in the cabin."

"I don't know where he went," Violet said. "But I know how he left the area without leaving any other footprints." She showed the others a path through the trees. There was a thick, smooth trail over the top snow. "Whoever that yeti is, he knows how to ride a snowboard." She pointed to a small bump in the snow where the snowboard tracks stopped. "The rider clearly jumped and then landed a few feet away," she said.

"I'm guessing most people who live around Hidden Hills can either snowboard or ski," Henry said. "I'm not sure that's a helpful clue."

"What about this?" Jessie trekked a few feet into the snow and picked up an extra large thermos. "Here's a helpful clue."

Henry took the thermos and opened it. There was a small amount of liquid inside. He poured the liquid into the snow. The snow immediately melted into a small puddle where the liquid hit. "Warm water." Henry put the lid back on the thermos. "It probably used to be very hot."

"A thirsty yeti?" Benny suggested.

Jessie wrote down the thermos in her notebook as a clue. "This thermos looks new." She turned it around in her hands. "No scratches or dents or anything."

"I think I'll also draw a map of the cabin and the snowboarding trail, and mark the spot where you found the thermos." Violet reached into her pocket for the drawing paper that Jessie had given her earlier. "Oh no," she said. "I left the paper near where we first saw the footprints."

"We can get it on the way down the mountain," Jessie said. "Do you want a clean page to draw something now?" Jessie pulled out her notebook.

"That's all right," Violet said. There was

a big recycling bin nearby. She lifted the lid and looked inside. "I can use any old scrap..." She took out a wrinkled piece of paper and smoothed it out. "Oh, look, it's one of Mr. Fellows's protest flyers." Violet studied the flyer and then turned her attention to the snowboard tracks.

"I'm just going to make a quick sketch of—" Violet turned over the flyer to draw on the back. "This is interesting. There's an advertisement for a local writing contest on the other side." After a quick read, she said, "It looks like Mr. Fellows edits a magazine when he's not serving coffee or yelling at hotel guests. They are hosting a competition, looking for essays about nature."

"He must have reused the paper," Jessie said. "Mr. Fellows told us to recycle the flyer when we were done reading it too. He's a good role model for saving the environment."

"I'm pretty sure he's also the yeti," Henry said, cutting into the conversation.

"You think Mr. Fellows is the yeti?" Benny asked, eyes wide. "Is he a shape-shifter?"

"Sorry, Benny, nothing supernatural. It looks like Mr. Fellows is a man dressing up like a yeti," Henry said. "The clues add up. The yeti footprints lead here. Mr. Fellows loves the environment, so I think he's living in this cabin in the woods." He pointed to the roof. "He's a recycling yeti who harnesses solar energy."

Jessie opened her notebook and looked at his name on the suspect list. "We already thought Mr. Fellows might have taken Clayton's snowboard to stop the competition..."

"And when the competition continued," Violet went on. "He dressed like the yeti and scared Patricia into falling."

"Coffee shop owner, writer, magazine editor, environmental protestor, snowboard thief..." Benny counted all the things Mr. Fellows did on his fingers. "He's too busy to be a yeti. I still think there's a real yeti."

"A yeti that snowboards?" Violet asked. "It's a good story, Benny, but I just don't think it's possible. That would be one amazing yeti." She drew a quick sketch of the snowboard track on the corner of the flyer and put it in her pocket. When they got back to the hotel, she'd tuck the page into her sketch pad.

Digging his toe in the snow, Benny said, "I was hoping there was a real yeti. Just one time, I'd like to find a live monster when we're solving a mystery, not just a person dressed like a monster." He frowned.

"Sorry, Benny," Jessie said, putting her arm around her brother. "No yeti. Not this time. We better go now and find Mr. Fellows before something bad happens to another snowboarder—"

Just then a scream came from the snowboarding course.

CHAPTER 6

Injured

The Aldens ran toward the shout.

They found Jasper lying in the snow, grasping his ankle.

Watch reached him first, followed close behind by Henry.

Being a sensitive dog, Watch put his nose up to Jasper's leg, as if he was a doctor checking the injury.

"I'm okay, boy," Jasper said, sitting up and giving Watch a pat on the head. He tried to stand, but he fell back down into the snow with a grunt. "Ouch."

"What happened?" Henry asked.

"Jasper twisted his ankle." Hyun was kneeling next to his friend, looking very concerned.

"You need to ice the injury immediately," Jessie said, scooping a small mound of snow and setting it onto his leg.

"Are you going to be able to compete?" Hyun asked.

Jasper took a moment to roll his foot around. "It hurts, but thanks to Jessie and this snow pack, it should heal really fast." He tried again to stand, but decided against getting up yet. "I think I'll sit here and rest for another few minutes."

Jessie set a fresh layer of snow over his injury. "Why were you up here on the mountain?"

Hyun answered, "When Patricia crashed, she dropped a mitten. The medical team took her away so fast they left it here. Since the chairlift is closed for the day, Jasper and I offered to hike up here to get it with her."

"We found it easily," Jasper said.

"We were about to go back down when Jasper tripped." Hyun pointed at a tree root that was sticking out of the snow. "The snow melted around the root, but Jasper didn't see it until he fell over it."

Violet stepped over the dangerous root and walked a few feet away. They were nearly in the same spot where she'd left the drawing paper so she went to get it. The page from Jessie's journal was wet and soggy. She put the paper in her pocket and began to step back to the others when she realized something important.

"Did you say that the snow around the root was melted?" Violet asked Hyun.

"Of course," Hyun said. "We see this all the time on the mountain. If the sun hits the snow and warms it, the snow turns to mush. There might be water around in little pools too." He took a fistful of snow and blew on it with his warm breath.

Jessie went to the root and stood near Violet. Together they examined the way the snow was melted. "Interesting," Jessie muttered.

"Roots are a hazard on any ski or snowboarding slope," Jasper said. "The snow covers the plants and earth below. It's scary when part of a tree sticks through—and can be really dangerous. A lot of places groom the slopes before winter to keep the plants from growing too much."

"Hidden Hills is known to be wild," Hyun said. "It's part of what makes boarding here so tricky."

"Once this place becomes Majestic Mountain," Jasper continued, "they'll have a lot more slopes—and they'll take better care of them."

Jessie looked around at the thick forest. "If they made more slopes, they'd probably need to cut down a lot of trees."

"Another reason to suspect Mr. Fellows," Henry said. "He would never want anyone to cut down the trees."

"Maybe it's time to go to the sheriff," Violet suggested. "I'm worried what might happen next."

"We can't accuse Mr. Fellows of anything

until we know more," Henry said. "We need real proof. We're still *guessing* he took Clayton's snowboard and we only *think* he is trying to scare the other snowboarders."

"We need to find out the truth," Jessie agreed.

Jasper said his ankle felt a lot better and he was able to stand up. Still he needed Henry and Hyun to help him down the mountain. Watch and Benny led the way to the medical clinic.

A nurse put Jasper in a room while another nurse filled out paperwork.

With a mystery still to solve, Henry, Jessie, Violet, and Benny decided to leave. They would come back and check on Jasper later.

As they headed to the door, they ran into Patricia.

"Are you all right?" Henry asked her.

"Yeah." She lifted the edge of her coat to show him her hip. A big black bruise had already begun to form.

"That looks nasty," Violet said, turning her head away.

"Athletes always get scrapes and bumps. This was small compared to some of my other crashes," Patricia said. "The doctor said I'm okay to snowboard in the final round tomorrow."

"What happened on the course today?" asked Jessie.

Patricia sighed. "I should have picked a less difficult spot to try to pass Mercedes." She shrugged. "I was going really fast and not paying attention to the surroundings. I fell over a tree root."

"You too?" Violet asked.

"What do you mean?"

"Jasper fell over a tree root and hurt his ankle looking for your missing glove," Jessie explained.

"Oh no!"

"He's okay," Henry told her. "Let's go see him."

Patricia and the Aldens returned to Jasper's room.

"Is it broken?" Patricia glanced at Jasper's ankle.

"Nah. The doctor wants me to stay here and ice it a bit longer, but I'm fine," Jasper assured her.

Patricia sighed in relief. "What's the news from the competition?" she asked her friends.

Hyun said, "Mercedes is first."

"Of course. I should have been able to pass her." Touching the bruised place on her own leg she moaned, "Rotten tree root."

"Are you sure the yeti didn't scare you and make you fall down during the race?" Benny asked.

"Yeti?" Patricia looked confused. "What are you talking about?"

Jessie explained, "We've been working on the mystery of Clayton's missing snowboard and we think Mr. Fellows has been dressing like a yeti to scare the snowboarders and get them to leave Hidden Hills."

"I don't understand," Patricia said. "I didn't see a yeti. I hit the root. That's why I fell."

"Hmmm." Jessie made a note in her journal.

"I came in second," Hyun continued, and he and Jasper high-fived.

Henry was impressed at how the snowboarders, while competing for slots at the camp, remained good friends who truly cared about one another.

"Jasper came in third today," Clayton said.

"That makes me fourth," Patricia said. "Drat."

"Better than fifth," Clayton grumped. "Don't forget who lost."

"You didn't lose," Patricia said. "You didn't race. We all know you'd have beaten us."

"Yeah," Clayton said with a chuckle. "You're right. I'd have beaten you all. Mercedes wouldn't have seen me as I blew past. I'd have been an orange-helmet blur."

Everyone laughed.

"We better go," Jessie whispered to Henry.

"Right," Henry replied. "We need to find Clayton's board before tomorrow's half-pipe."

The half-pipe was the most exciting, and most dangerous, event. It was when Clayton would show off his move: the Hollow.

"I added something different to the Hollow," Clayton told the others. "I'm going to give the move a brand new name."

"Is it another spin?" Hyun asked. "I dream about rotating my board as fast as you do yours."

Clayton zipped his lips and didn't say.

"I bet it's a grab," Patricia said. That was when a snowboarder grabbed the edge of the board in a trick.

Clayton kept his lips tightly shut.

"I can't wait!" Benny said. "Let's find Clayton's board so he can do the new trick." He looked at Clayton and asked, "You could call it the Benny!"

"Find my board, and I'll name it after you for sure," Clayton told him.

"Let's hurry!" Benny tugged on Jessie's hand. Then he stopped and let her go. "Wait. Before we find the board, you promised linner." His tummy growled. "I can't possibly solve this mystery with a grumbly tummy."

"Okay," agreed Henry. "But let's make a

quick stop at the hotel first. We should let Grandfather know where we are."

As the Aldens were about to leave the clinic, the doctor came and told Jasper he could go.

"I'd like to get something to eat with you, Benny." Jasper rubbed his own belly. "I'm starving."

"Burger Bonanza?" Patricia asked. "We can all go."

Clayton shook his head. "I'll go with you to hang out, but I won't eat. The food is awful."

"It's not bad if you're very, very hungry," Jasper said.

"'Not bad' sounds good to me," Benny said, putting on his gloves and hat for the walk.

Just outside the clinic, Mercedes was talking to her coach.

"We're going to Burger Bonanza," Henry called out to her. "You can come if you want."

Mercedes gave Henry a blank look that he didn't understand. Her eyes seemed sad, even though she'd won both races that day.

"Do you think she heard me?" Henry asked. They were a few feet away.

"She looked at you," Benny said. "I think she heard you but can't talk because she's meeting with her scary coach."

"He's probably yelling at her for not being faster than lightening," Jessie whispered to Violet.

Violet was about to agree when it became clear that the coach wasn't yelling at Mercedes. She was yelling at the coach.

"No!" She threw a dripping wet Burger Bonanza ski cap at him and stomped away. He ducked and it landed in the snow.

Coach McNaught picked it up and caught up with her. He said something the children couldn't hear.

Mercedes's face turned red. "No one is listening to me! No one ever asks what I want!" She reached into her pocket and this time, threw a wadded-up piece of paper at the coach. "I want to win! And I want it so much, I'll do anything." She sneered at him and repeated, "I'll win. You'll see."

Mercedes stormed off in a huff.

"Yikes," Benny said. "Mercedes is scary when she's angry."

"I wonder…" Henry was quiet for a second then said to Jessie, "Mr. Fellows might have taken Clayton's board, but now I'm wondering if we need to research another suspect too."

"Mercedes?" Jessie asked, opening her notebook. "I'm not sure how she would have gotten it. She was with us when the board disappeared."

"Was she?" Violet asked. "I don't remember her standing at the scoreboard."

"I saw her by the fence, after she got her snowboard," Benny said. "I think she only took the pink one."

"And her ski hat was wet," Violet said. "She might have melted the snow and dropped the hat in the puddle."

"Can any of us be absolutely sure Mercedes didn't have a chance to steal the snowboard? Or at least hide it somewhere she could come back to later and get it?" Henry asked them all.

No one answered.

"I guess it's possible," Jessie said, writing down Mercedes's name in her journal.

"She just made it clear she'd do anything to win," Violet said. "Maybe that means cheating."

"But Mercedes couldn't be the yeti," Jessie said.

Henry shrugged. "Maybe the yeti and the snowboard aren't related. I have to think more about it and—"

"Let's think more while we eat," Benny suggested. "Come on."

The snowboarders had gone ahead of them. Benny ran to catch up.

"Hang on, Henry." Violet went back to the place where Mercedes and her coach had been fighting. "I don't want to leave trash around." Violet picked up the rumpled paper that Mercedes had thrown at her coach. It was Mr. Fellows's protest flyer. Violet smoothed it out and reviewed the advertisement for the writing competition on the back.

"I'm impressed he used both sides," she said, thinking about the flyers again. "This

is all a little confusing to me. Mr. Fellows might be the bad guy here, but he really cares about the environment, and that makes him a good person too."

"It really is complicated, isn't it?" Henry remarked while he lifted the lid on a nearby recycling container.

"Mysteries are never easy," Jessie agreed.

CHAPTER 7

Suspect Number One

When the Aldens arrived at the hotel, they noticed the lobby was a mess. Chairs were knocked over, a broken table lay near a smashed vase, and Mr. Fellows's protest flyers were scattered in every corner like oversized confetti.

Henry held the others back. "I'm not sure it's safe to go inside," he said, searching for the sheriff.

Jessie saw the sheriff interviewing a well-dressed couple by the front desk.

Henry went to the front desk and asked the manager, "What happened here?"

"Mr. Fellows came in here complaining about the winter sports camp and handing his flyers to all the hotel guests." She looked back over the damage and sighed. "I asked him to leave and reminded him this is private property. This time, he agreed to go away."

"How'd everything get broken then?" Jessie asked.

"Coach McNaught came downstairs from his room as Mr. Fellows was leaving. He approached him and they began to argue," she explained.

She bent down to pick up a piece of broken glass and held it tenderly in her hands. "I know Ralph. We both grew up here. Sometimes he gets emotional. I understand why he threw paint on the plans for Majestic Mountain this morning. He's mad about the development."

"I noticed how quickly the paint was cleaned up," Henry remarked.

"Typical Ralph. It was an environmental blend," Martha told him. "Cleaned up easy with soap and water." She shook her head. "He might mess up some big international company's drawings to protest what they're doing, but he'd never break my grandmother's vase on purpose."

"I'm guessing Mr. Fellows would be upset about the waste as well," Violet added. "The plant that was in that vase is dead now." She pointed out the dirt and leaves that were part of the chaos on the floor.

Just then a car drove up to the front of the building. "Oh no!" The manager moaned. "It's a bad time for new guests to arrive. I better go and greet them." She hurried outside to the parking area.

Jessie leaned into Henry and whispered, "Look there." Dirt footprints were on the floor; they went behind the front registration desk and through a doorway at the back. "I think Mr. Fellows is hiding in the hotel."

Henry looked at the footprints.

Henry told Violet, and she showed Benny the clue.

Tiptoeing past the sheriff, Benny led the

way behind the desk. He opened the door to the office and saw that there was another door that led to the alleyway.

"This way," Jessie said. At the end of the alley was a florist shop with a greenhouse in back. Jessie had a feeling that Mr. Fellows would go somewhere that was full of plants and green things.

"Let's be careful," Henry said as he opened the greenhouse door. "We don't know if Mr. Fellows is dangerous or not."

Violet shook her head. "I've been thinking a lot about him. I just don't think he's a bad man. I think we've read the clues wrong."

"We need to find out more," Henry said.

They approached Mr. Fellows together.

He was standing between two long rows of little plants that were being warmed by artificial lights. When he saw the children, Mr. Fellows raised his arms in surrender. "I want to replace the plant from the broken vase," he said. "After I clean up the mess and apologize, you can take me to jail."

"Detectives don't arrest anyone," Benny

told him. "We have to call the sheriff to come get you."

"Detectives?" Mr. Fellows asked, lowering his arms and crossing them over his chest. "Is there a mystery to solve?" He shivered.

"Do you know what happened to Clayton Hollow's snowboard?" Henry asked.

"Is it missing?" Mr. Fellows wrinkled his eyebrows then asked, "Who is Clayton Hollow?"

"You don't know?" Benny walked over to Mr. Fellows and looked closely in his face. "Are you joking around?"

"No." Mr. Fellows shrugged.

"He's one of the snowboarders in the competition," Jessie told him. "His snowboard disappeared yesterday and we're trying to help him get it back."

"Are you positive you didn't take it?" Benny asked.

"Yes. I'm sure I didn't take anything." Mr. Fellows looked hard at Benny. "I mean, I don't want the mountain town to grow, but I'm not a thief. I don't even know how to snowboard.

I'm just handing out my flyers and discussing the issues."

"We followed a yeti's footprints to your cabin," Violet said. "We thought you were trying to scare the snowboarders away from Hidden Hills."

"A yeti?" Mr. Fellows shook his head. "What yeti?"

"Aren't you dressing up as the yeti?" Benny's eyes grew wide.

"No." He was confused. "What are you talking about?"

"Ha!" Benny jumped up and down. "If he's not the yeti, that means it's real! I knew the yeti was real! A real yeti!" He was very excited.

Just then, the Aldens and Mr. Fellows could hear voices from the street. "I hope they have recycling bins in the jailhouse."

"I didn't do anything wrong, you know," Mr. Fellows told the Aldens. "That big gorilla wants the training camp to be here. When I gave him a flyer, he attacked me." He frowned. "Unfortunately, I broke Martha's grandmother's vase trying to escape his grip. I hope she'll forgive me."

"I have a feeling she will," Violet said.

"I don't understand," Mr. Fellows said. "Just a few hours ago, Coach McNaught came to the Coffee Hut complaining he was cold. He bought a reusable insulated coffee cup. I filled it with hot water to heat him up. That's what I drink when I'm cold. He seemed happy when he left the shop." He pinched his lips together. "When I saw him in the hotel lobby, I thought he'd read my flyer and we could have a conversation. Instead he tried to hit me."

The voices in the alley grew louder. They were just outside the greenhouse. "Ralph? Are you in there?" It was the hotel manager.

"I'm here," he said.

"Come on out," she told him. "We've watched the security video from the lobby. We know you didn't do anything wrong."

"I don't have to go to jail?" he shouted out.

"This time you have to promise to stop holding your protests in the hotel. You can't mention Majestic Mountain or hand out flyers when you're on my turf. You have your own coffee shop. Protest there all you want."

"Oh, fine. I think everyone knows my opinion anyway. I'm on my way." Mr. Fellows quickened his steps as he neared the door. "Hey, Martha, don't let anyone touch the mess. I'll clean it all up by myself."

"Why won't you let anyone else clean up?" Violet asked, though she guessed the answer.

"This town is run by people who want development—more people coming around and making more trash. They don't care. All those tourists and sporting kids will put glass in with paper and plastic with the compost!" he said. "No one knows how to use the recycling bins correctly. This town *needs* me."

Violet smiled. "That's what I figured. We know how to recycle too. Want some help?"

Henry, Jessie, and Benny agreed.

"We're good helpers," Benny said.

"I'd appreciate it," Mr. Fellows said. "Thanks."

As they went back to the hotel, Henry asked Jessie, "Who's next on our suspect list?"

"There are two names left. Ms. Taylor and Mercedes. I think we should find Ms. Taylor," Jessie said. "We need to go to Burger Bonanza."

"Jessie!" Benny shouted up at his sister. "There are three suspects left, not two— three! Ms. Taylor. Mercedes. And the yeti. Don't forget about the yeti!"

CHAPTER 8

Burgers and Lies

When the hotel lobby was clean, Jessie sat on the chair and opened her notebook. She crossed off Mr. Fellows's name.

"I'm too hungry to keep solving mysteries," Benny said, lying down on the couch. "I feel faint!"

"The snowboarders are all at the Burger Bonanza," Jessie said. "We can meet them there and check out Ms. Taylor at the same time."

At that, Benny jumped off the couch and hustled out the hotel and onto the street.

"He's not faint anymore," Violet said as she ran after him toward the Burger Bonanza.

Grandfather had brought Watch to the lobby so Jessie could take him along. She fed him dog treats while Ms. Taylor led the children to a large table in the back of the restaurant. The snowboarders were there busy talking about the competition.

"We waited for you," Patricia told Benny. "Just like we promised."

"Thanks!" He sat in an empty chair between her and Jasper. "What do you recommend?" Benny asked Ms. Taylor.

"The Burger Bonanza Bonanza of course," she replied, casting a quick glance toward Clayton. "It's a double big burger for a big belly."

Benny rubbed his tummy. "I'll take two!" he said. "I'm starving."

Jessie laughed. "One Bonanza is plenty for Benny. And a side of fruit please."

"I like fruit," Benny said, licking his lips. "Delicious."

"Oh we don't serve fruit," Ms. Taylor said, "But he can have French fries."

"I told you," Clayton leaned in and whispered. "It's not that the food tastes terrible, it's that there's nothing healthy here. They don't even put lettuce or tomato on the burger. There isn't a fresh vegetable in the whole place."

Jessie swore she heard Ms. Taylor snarl, but when she looked up, the Bonanza owner was all smiles.

"I'll take a Bonanza Bonanza too," Jasper said.

"Double Bonanza Burgers for everyone, then?" Ms. Taylor asked the crowd.

"Not for me," Clayton told her. "I'll just have water."

"What is wrong with you?" Ms. Taylor was suddenly angry. "It should be an honor to wear the Burger Bonanza hats and snowboard on a Burger Bonanza board! When you advertise for me, I'll give the camp money. We all win."

"We've gone through this before. I think the food is bad for you and I won't represent a product I don't believe in," Clayton said with a casual shrug. "Sorry. But that's how I feel." He added, "And if I make the camp, the group has to vote unanimously on who the sponsor will be."

"I hope you don't come to camp." Ms. Taylor glared at Clayton. She repeated what she'd said before on the slope, the first time the Aldens had met her. "I hope you *never* find your snowboard." With a mighty huff, she stormed off to the front counter.

Clayton turned to Henry. "Is she a suspect? I mean, she doesn't want me to succeed and she keeps saying she hopes Bessie is gone forever." He glanced toward the cash register where Ms. Taylor was helping another customer. "Seems pretty clear to me she must be the thief."

Jessie opened her notebook and showed him the page. "She's on the list."

"Who else are you investigating?" Clayton asked.

"Mercedes might have taken your board," Henry answered.

"No way!" Clayton exclaimed. "Impossible. We're friends."

"She told her coach she'd do *anything* to win," Jessie said. "She knows you are a really good snowboarder, so we think she might be trying to get you out to guarantee a slot for herself."

"No way," Clayton repeated. "Mercedes would never do that." He looked around the table. "Are Hyun, Jasper, and Patricia suspects too?"

Jessie pinched her lips. "No." She thought about it. "They were all with us at the scoreboard when Bessie disappeared."

"So was Mercedes," Clayton said. Then he paused, "Wasn't she?"

"That's the problem," Henry said. "We can't seem to remember."

Clayton sat quietly. "I don't think it's Mercedes, but maybe you should keep checking." His eyes showed that he'd be very sad if she was the one. He really liked Mercedes and trusted her. "I want Bessie back."

Ms. Taylor brought their food and set it on the table. She gave everyone Burger Bonanza stickers, even Clayton. "Maybe you'll change your mind about the restaurant," she said before walking away.

Benny poured ketchup on his burger and then smelled it. "Mmmm." He opened his mouth to take a big bite then suddenly set the burger down.

"What's wrong?" Violet asked. "That burger was almost in your tummy."

"I know," Benny said. "But I thought of something and I had to tell you right away."

"What?" Jessie and Henry asked at the same time.

"Ms. Taylor is lying," Benny said. "Clayton isn't the only one who doesn't want Burger Bonanza as a sponsor." He explained, "I don't think Mercedes would like riding a Burger board either."

"We saw her throw the restaurant's hat at her coach," Violet recalled. "I thought it was because she was mad."

"She's a vegetarian," Benny said. "I offered her beef jerky and she told me she doesn't eat meat." He picked a sesame seed off his burger bun.

Henry asked Clayton, "Have you ever talked to Mercedes about the sponsorship?"

"No," Clayton admitted. "I never thought about it."

Jessie took out her pen. "As long as Mercedes gets to be part of the camp, there will be a vote against Burger Bonanza sponsoring the snowboarders."

"I don't think Ms. Taylor is a suspect anymore," Violet said. "If Clayton isn't the only one against her, she's got no reason to steal *his* board."

"Maybe she doesn't know Mercedes is a vegetarian," Benny suggested. He put down his burger and stood up. "I'll get her so we can ask."

Benny returned a minute later with Ms. Taylor. "Is something wrong?" she wanted to know.

"Mercedes doesn't eat meat," Benny told her. "So we just figured out that Clayton isn't the only one who doesn't want to advertise for the restaurant."

"I'm willing to pay a lot of money to the camp," Ms. Taylor said. "Coach McNaught promised me he will talk to Mercedes about it and get her to change her mind. She doesn't have to eat burgers to wear the restaurant's name on her stuff." She turned to Clayton, "You don't have to eat here either, but it would be better if you did."

Clayton looked Ms. Taylor in the eye. "Did you steal my snowboard?"

She looked shocked. "What?" Then her face softened. "Of course not. If you're going to represent Burger Bonanza, I need you to win. Everyone knows Clayton Hollow can't win without his board, Yellow Bessie."

"But you keep saying you hope he never finds Bessie," Benny said.

"I'm just saying that because I'm mad about the sponsorship. That's all."

"So you didn't take my board to force me to use yours?" Clayton asked. "Or to keep me out of the camp?"

"Not my style," Ms. Taylor told him. "I want to win your heart with my food." She snapped her fingers and a waiter brought a burger to the table. He set it in front of Clayton. "This one is for you. It's free. I hope you'll change your mind and *want* to represent it." She walked away.

When she was gone, Clayton peeked under the bun. "Not even a pickle," he said, pushing the burger away. "One little wrinkled vegetable, is that too much to ask?"

"A cucumber is a fruit." Henry laughed.

"I'd accept that," Clayton said. "Anything is better than deep fried onions and goopy cheese."

"Sounds yummy to me," Benny said, picking up his burger again.

"You can take Ms. Taylor off the suspect list," Violet told Jessie.

While Jessie crossed off her name, Benny took a big bite of burger. He slowly chewed and swallowed. Then he set the rest of the burger down on the plate. "I've eaten a million hamburgers and I've never had one like this," he said. Benny wrinkled his nose. "Clayton's right. This hamburger tastes unhealthy! Clayton shouldn't use Ms. Taylor's snowboard or wear her hat. I wouldn't advertise for her either." He looked at his belly and said, "I'll find you something yummy and good for you later. Sorry, tummy."

The Aldens left the restaurant without finishing their meal.

"That only leaves Mercedes's name on the suspect list," Henry said. "I really hope she didn't do it."

"We still have another suspect—the yeti." Benny was frustrated that he had to keep reminding everyone. "It's still possible he's the thief."

"We'll check him out next," Jessie assured Benny.

The Aldens were on their way back to the hotel when the hotel manager came running up to them. "Have you seen Mercedes?" she asked, out of breath.

"We were heading to her room to talk to her now," Henry said. "Why?"

"Because I just went to deliver a package that came for her." She held up a big brown envelope. "Her coach was in the room with her mom and they were very upset."

"What's going on?" Jessie asked. "Do you know?"

"I heard them talking." Martha lowered the envelope and said, "Mercedes ran away."

CHAPTER 9

The Snowboard Thief

By morning, there was still no sign of Mercedes, but the officials for the snowboarding competition declared that the half-pipe was to go on as planned.

Hyun, Patricia, and Jasper looked frustrated and concerned as they climbed onto the chairlift up the mountain.

Clayton didn't even get dressed for the race. "Strange," Clayton said as he stood with the Aldens in the viewing area. "There are four slots for the training camp, and now only three competitors." He looked over his shoulder at the scoreboard, where the ranks were posted. "Mercedes will still beat me, even if she doesn't snowboard today. Her rank is higher." He sighed then said, "Wherever she is, I hope she's all right."

Benny had convinced Jessie to get him a cup of hot chocolate before coming to watch the three competitors. He took a sip and said, "The half-pipe is the most exciting event. It's when the riders get to show off their best tricks." He took another long drink of cocoa. "I just don't feel like watching today."

Watch groaned and hung his head low as if to agree.

Violet took out a piece of paper and drew a quick sketch of the slope. Light snow was falling, so she etched in the flakes with light touches of her pencil. "The day is bright, but it feels so gray," she said.

Everyone was feeling bad about Clayton's board and wondering where Mercedes had gone.

Hyun was the first boarder down the

mountain. The mood lifted just a little as he slid from side to side in the large half-pipe for the competition. He grabbed the front of his board and ended with a double flip.

Benny stood up to cheer. He forgot about his hot chocolate and spilled it over the edge of the viewing benches. "Oh no," he groaned. "Not again!"

Jessie stared down as the brown liquid heated and melted the snow, just like the first time, leaving a tree root showing and a puddle of melted water.

Benny stumbled forward and dropped his hat into the puddle. The water made his ski cap wet.

"Melted snow," she said out loud as she scooped up Benny's dripping hat.

"A puddle of water." Henry was standing next to her. He looked at the ground and repeated, "Melted water!"

"Of course!" Violet put down her art. "We have to go."

"I think we all know who the thief is," Henry said.

"And here is the final clue." Benny shook his wet hat.

Up on the slope, Patricia's name was announced as the next one to do tricks in the half-pipe.

"Hurry," Benny told Clayton and pointed to the hotel. "Meet us at the chairlift when you're ready. We're going to find your snowboard."

"You solved the mystery?" Clayton didn't move. He wrinkled his eyebrows. "Just now?"

"No guarantee," Henry told him. "But we think we know who took it. There might not be enough time to get the board and come back before your turn, but we're going to try."

Jessie took Watch's leash and the two of them jumped from the benches.

"You should get ready," Violet told Clayton. "We'll see you soon."

The Aldens rushed to the hotel and went directly to Mercedes's room. Henry knocked.

Her mother, Mrs. Moon, opened the door. Her long brown hair was a tangled mess and her eyes were red from staying up all night worrying. "Have you seen Mercedes?" she asked.

"No," Jessie said. "We're looking for Coach McNaught."

"I heard you were young detectives," Mercedes's mother said. "Can you help find her? Tell her she never has to snowboard again if she doesn't want to. I just want her to come home."

Hearing that, Coach McNaught came out of the adjoining hotel room. "What? Never snowboard again?" He stomped into the room toward Mrs. Moon with an angry expression on his face. "What are you talking about? Of course she must snowboard. She has no choice. She will be an international champion!"

"Hi." Benny waved at the coach and calmly asked, "Can we please have Clayton's snowboard? We're in a hurry."

"I don't know what you're talking about." The coach stared at Benny.

"You see," Benny explained, "if Clayton

can do his new trick in the half-pipe, he'll name it after me. So we need Yellow Bessie back now."

"I don't have Clayton Hollow's snowboard," the coach said, putting his hands on his hips and standing tall. Benny moved away. Coach McNaught was a really big man.

"The clues brought us here," Jessie said, opening her notebook. "You weren't at the scoreboard after the first race, so you could have easily taken it."

"We saw a large figure that looked like a yeti on the mountain near where Patricia crashed," Henry continued. "The snow had been melted around a root that made her fall."

Jessie picked up the story. "You gave Mercedes the wet Burger Bonanza hat, which she threw at you. She doesn't want to wear their clothes or sponsor that restaurant."

"The hat was wet because you dropped it when you melted the snow." Benny held up his own soggy ski cap. "You used hot water you got at the Coffee Hut in a brand-new thermos."

"After you made the dangerous tree root pop out of the snow, you rushed to Mr. Fellows's cabin and accidentally dropped the thermos when you snowboarded away from there." Henry explained how they'd seen the snowboard tracks, and how Mr. Fellows said he didn't know how to snowboard. "You are a snowboarding champion. That's how you got down the mountain so fast."

"There was only one set of footprints," Benny said with a pout, "because *you* are the yeti." He leaned toward Henry and said, "It was a disguise. I bet he even has a furry coat. He wanted to trick us so we wouldn't think he was a suspect." He stared at the coach's giant yeti-like feet. "No yeti." Benny huffed, "I knew it all along."

"One more thing," Jessie added. "You started a fight in the hotel lobby with Mr. Fellows so that everyone would think he was a bad guy and blame him for everything. No one would even think you might be the thief."

"Is it true?" Mrs. Moon turned to the coach. "Did you do all this?"

Coach McNaught snarled at the Aldens. "My reputation is at stake. I've been training Mercedes for years. If she doesn't make the elite snowboard training camp, I will be laughed at. I will never get another job! She must win a spot."

Mercedes's mother put her hands over her face. "I have such a headache. I've been terrible to my daughter." She began to cry. "She asked to quit. I wouldn't let her. She wanted a break. I said no. I told her she had to win." The woman looked up at the coach and pushed her hair off her face. "I've made a big mistake." She glared at the coach. "If you have the snowboard, you better give it to them right away."

Coach McNaught sighed and went to his own room. Jessie heard a closet open and when he returned, he was carrying Bessie. Henry took it from the coach.

"You're fired," Mercedes's mother said.

"We need to run," Jessie told them both. "We'll talk to the sheriff after the race. Clayton deserves a chance to compete today."

"When we get back," Henry said, "we can help find Mercedes." Then suddenly, he had an idea. The envelope the hotel manager had delivered for Mercedes was sitting on the table. "Maybe there's a clue inside," Henry said. "Can we open it?"

Mrs. Moon agreed and Jessie carefully slid a letter out of the envelope. "It's an invitation to a prestigious writing program in Montana," Jessie said. "Did you know Mercedes wants to be a writer?" she asked Mrs. Moon.

"I did," she said. "But Coach McNaught told me that she was being ridiculous. Once she got a spot at the training camp, she'd realize that writing wasn't her real dream, going to the International Games would be her dream." She shook her head. "I agreed that she should continue to snowboard."

Violet opened her sketch pad. She'd stuck Mr. Fellows's protest flyer inside the cover. "I think this might be the answer," she said, tapping the page with her finger. Henry turned the page over.

"She threw this flyer at you, Coach," Henry

said. "And shouted that she'd win, no matter what."

"We thought she meant she'd win at the snowboarding competition," Benny said. "But it wasn't that at all."

"She wanted to win the writing contest!" Violet declared.

Jessie put everything together. "We know where Mercedes is," she said. "She's with Mr. Fellows at the Coffee Hut."

"I'll go right away," Mrs. Moon told them. "I have to apologize to her."

"We better get Yellow Bessie to the slope," Henry said. "Clayton is going to be very happy."

"This mystery is solved," Violet said. "Case of the missing snowboard—closed."

"And missing Mercedes," Benny added. "We closed that case too."

"Good work," Henry told his siblings.

Then, tucking Bessie under his arm, Henry led the way out the hotel to the bottom of the chairlift where Clayton was waiting.

CHAPTER 10

The Amazing Aldens

Clayton's eyes lit up when he saw the Aldens headed his way. "Bessie!" he shouted.

"Tighten your helmet," Henry said. "We want to see some tricks."

"The Benny!" Benny said. "You promised."

"I think," Clayton said with a huge smile, "I'll call my new move the Amazing Aldens."

"That's even better!" Benny gave Clayton a high-five.

"I want to hear how you solved the

mystery," Clayton said as he moved toward the chairlift.

"We'll tell you everything later," Jessie called out. "Good luck."

As the chairlift moved toward the top of the mountain, a cheer erupted from the viewing area. Jasper had just finished his turn in the half-pipe.

The announcer said he would be the last snowboarder for the day.

"No!" Benny shouted. "There's one more." He jumped up and down, pointing at the chairlift.

"Oh no. We're too late—" Violet began when suddenly a new announcement came over the loudspeakers.

"Clayton Hollow appears to be on his way up the slope." The speakers went quiet for a moment. "We've checked the rules and because he wasn't here at the start of the event, he's not allowed to compete."

A roar came from the viewing stands. The audience began to chant, "Let him board!"

"Let him board!" Benny recited with them.

The speakers went silent again before the announcer came back on once more. "It seems there is a new development. Mercedes Moon, even without doing today's half-pipe, would have still taken a spot at the training camp. But—"

It sounded like there was a scuffle in the announcing booth, then Mercedes's voice came over the speakers. "I am no longer a snowboarder. I'm giving up my board and going to a writing program in Montana. Clayton can have my spot at camp." At first the shocked crowd was quiet. Then when they realized Mercedes was very happy with her choice, they cheered.

A man shouted, "We want to see his new trick!"

"Yes!" Jessie and Violet cheered louder than anyone in all of Hidden Hills. Henry clapped until his hands hurt. Watch barked. And Benny punched the air, shouting "Yay!"

In an excited voice, Mercedes Moon announced, "So here he is, my close friend,

Clayton Hollow, riding on Yellow Bessie. Watch out for the Awesome Aldens!"

Clayton appeared on the edge of the half-pipe. He pushed himself over the edge and did some slow moves to start. He sprang off the tail of the board then rotated backward and grabbed the board with both hands. He performed a fantastic spin.

Jasper came to stand next to Henry and identified a few other moves: Swiss Cheese Air, Chicken Salad, and Roast Beef.

"I love snowboarding!" Benny shouted, rubbing his tummy. "It's delicious."

The crowd went silent as Clayton stood for a moment at the edge of the long drop into the pipe.

As he picked up speed, he raised one foot off the board. Tucking his free leg under himself, Clayton bent low into a cannonball, then flipped the board over twice. He grabbed the edge of the board with both hands, got his foot back into the binding, and triple flipped before making a perfect landing.

He slid down the mountain and stopped right in front of the Aldens.

"Did you like it?" He was breathing heavily and his face was flushed.

"It was great!" Henry said.

"Perfect," Violet agreed.

"Fantastic," Jessie put in.

"How'd you do that?" Benny asked while the crowd went crazy, shouting and stomping.

Clayton laughed. He gave Benny a big hug and winked. "It's a mystery."

* * *

Grandfather met the children at the hotel. The car was packed and ready for the return trip to Greenfield.

The hotel manager came out to thank Henry, Jessie, Violet, and Benny. "Coach McNaught was arrested for stealing the board. You were right about Mercedes too. She was in the Coffee Hut showing Mr. Fellows her essay."

Mercedes, her mom, and Mr. Fellows came out of the hotel just then.

"I didn't want to come back to the hotel,"

Mercedes explained. "I was afraid you'd make me snowboard. I told Mr. Fellows you said it was okay if I worked on the essay all night."

"We're sorry everyone was worried," Mr. Fellows said. "I didn't know everyone thought she was missing."

"I'm so grateful to have my daughter back safely," said Mrs. Moon. "I'll never make Mercedes follow someone else's dream. I've learned an important lesson this weekend." She put a hand on Mercedes's shoulder. "When we get home, you'll be in trouble for staying out all night."

Mercedes frowned.

"But," her mom continued, "from now on, we are going to be honest with each other about everything. That way, we can make important decisions together."

"Yes," Mercedes agreed. "It's best to be honest."

They all moved aside as Clayton came through the group. "Come back any time," he told the Aldens. "The training camp is going to be held here after all."

"It is?" Jessie looked at Mr. Fellows.

"I made a deal with Ms. Taylor," Mr. Fellows explained. "One sports program will come at a time, so there aren't too many people at once. There will be an orientation class on protecting the environment and how to use recycling bins." He put an arm around Clayton. "And she promised a new menu for her snowboarders. The Burger Bonanza will now be the Healthy Habit, serving organic meat and using locally grown fruits and vegetables." Mr. Fellows shrugged. "I know it won't be perfect at first. It takes time for people to adjust to clean living, but Hidden Hills is going to be a model community."

"I'm writing my first article for Mr. Fellows's magazine on ways the town can reuse the old mining cabins," Mercedes said. "He's paying me. I'll be a real reporter!"

"Everything worked out, then." Henry was very glad. "We'll make a plan to come back as soon as we can," he told Clayton.

"It didn't *all* work out," Benny grumped.

"There was no yeti."

"I made this for you." Violet gave Benny a drawing she'd created of a yeti standing on the mountain.

"It's good," he said. "Thanks, Violet. I just wish we'd found a real yeti."

"There might not be a yeti, Benny," Mr. Fellows said, "but there is an old silver miner's ghost in one of the cabins on the mountain. Come back to visit and I'll introduce you."

Benny got very excited. "Let's stay!" He looked at Grandfather. "Can we? Just one night?"

Grandfather put his hand on Benny's head. "We've all had enough excitement in Hidden Hills," he said. "It's time to go home."

Benny climbed into the backseat of Grandfather's car and rolled down the window. His warm breath was visible in the frozen air. "We'll be back," he shouted to everyone at the hotel as the car pulled away. "Tell the ghost that I can't wait to meet him!"

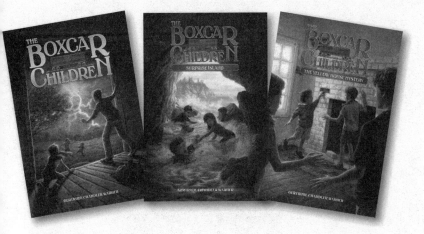

For more about the Boxcar Children,
visit them online at

TheBoxcarChildren.com

THE BOXCAR CHILDREN BEGINNING

by Patricia MacLachlan

Before they were the Boxcar Children, Henry, Jessie, Violet, and Benny Alden lived with their parents on Fair Meadow Farm.

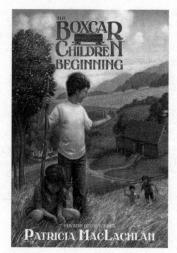

978-0-8075-6617-6
US $5.99 paperback

Although times are hard, they're happy—"the best family of all," Mama likes to say. And when a traveling family needs shelter from a winter storm, the Aldens help, and make new friends. But the spring and summer bring events that will change all their lives forever.

Newbery Award-winning author Patricia MacLachlan tells a wonderfully moving story of the Alden children's origins.

* * *

"Fans will enjoy this picture of life 'before.'"—*Publishers Weekly*

"An approachable lead-in that serves to fill in the background both for confirmed fans and readers new to the series." —*Kirkus Reviews*

THE BOXCAR CHILDREN SPOOKTACULAR SPECIAL

created by Gertrude Chandler Warner

Three spooky stories in one big book!

From ghosts to zombies to a haunting in their very own backyard, the Boxcar Children have plenty of spooktacular adventures in these three exciting mysteries.

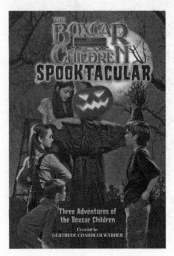

978-0-8075-7605-2
US $9.99 paperback

THE ZOMBIE PROJECT
The story about the Winding River zombie is just an old legend. But Benny sees a strange figure lurching through the woods and thinks the zombie could be real!

THE MYSTERY OF THE HAUNTED BOXCAR
One night the Aldens see a mysterious light shining inside the boxcar where they once lived. Soon they discover spooky new clues to the old train car's past!

THE PUMPKIN HEAD MYSTERY
Every year the Aldens help out with the fun at a pumpkin farm. Can they find out why a ghost with a jack-o'-lantern head is haunting the hayrides?

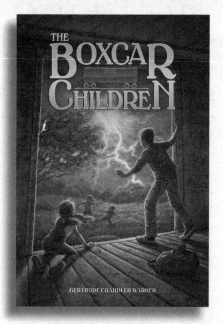

#1 THE BOXCAR CHILDREN
THE BOXCAR CHILDREN® MYSTERIES
HC 978-0-8075-0851-0
$15.99/$17.99 Canada
PB 978-0-8075-0852-7
$5.99/$6.99 Canada
"One warm night four children stood in front of a bakery. No one knew them. No one knew where they had come from." So begins Gertrude Chandler Warner's beloved story about four orphans who run away and find shelter in an abandoned boxcar. There they manage to live all on their own, and at last, find love and security from an unexpected source.

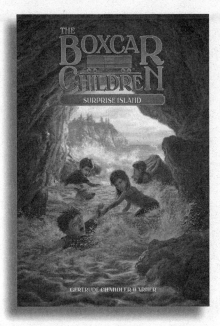

#2 SURPRISE ISLAND
THE BOXCAR CHILDREN® MYSTERIES
HC 978-0-8075-7673-1
$15.99/$17.99 Canada
PB 978-0-8075-7674-8
$5.99/$6.99 Canada
The Boxcar Children have a home with their
grandfather now—but their adventures are just
beginning! Their first adventure is to spend the
summer camping on their own private island.
The island is full of surprises, including a kind
stranger with a secret.

#3 THE YELLOW HOUSE MYSTERY
THE BOXCAR CHILDREN® MYSTERIES
HC 978-0-8075-9365-3
$15.99/$17.99 Canada
PB 978-0-8075-9366-0
$5.99/$6.99 Canada
Henry, Jessie, Violet, and Benny Alden discover
that a mystery surrounds the rundown yellow
house on Surprise Island. The children find a
letter and other clues that lead them to the trail
of a man who vanished from the house.

#4 MYSTERY RANCH
THE BOXCAR CHILDREN® MYSTERIES
HC 978-0-8075-5390-9
$15.99/$17.99 Canada
PB 978-0-8075-5391-6
$5.99/$6.99 Canada
Henry, Jessie, Violet, and Benny Alden just
found out they have an Aunt Jane and travel out
west to spend the summer on her ranch. While
there, they make an amazing discovery about
the ranch that will change Aunt Jane's life.

GERTRUDE CHANDLER WARNER discovered when she was teaching that many readers who like an exciting story could find no books that were both easy and fun to read. She decided to try to meet this need, and her first book, *The Boxcar Children*, quickly proved she had succeeded.

Miss Warner drew on her own experiences to write the mystery. As a child she spent hours watching trains go by on the tracks opposite her family home. She often dreamed about what it would be like to set up housekeeping in a caboose or freight car—the situation the Alden children find themselves in.

While the mystery element is central to each of Miss Warner's books, she never thought of them as strictly juvenile mysteries. She liked to stress the Aldens' independence and resourcefulness and their solid New England devotion to using up and making do. The Aldens go about most of their adventures with as little adult supervision as possible— something else that delights young readers.

Miss Warner lived in Putnam, Connecticut, until her death in 1979. During her lifetime, she received hundreds of letters from girls and boys telling her how much they liked her books.